Love Burns

Drahgue Dragon No. 1
A Sweet Paranormal Romance

By

Josette Reuel

Love Burns: Drahgue Dragon 1

Copyright c) 2017 Josette Reuel
Cover design by Evanlea Designs
Proofreading and Edits: Evanlea Publishing and Reuel's Rebels' Beta Crew.

All rights reserved. No part of this book may be reproduced in any form or by any electronic or mechanical means including information storage and retrieval systems – except in the case of brief quotations embodied in critical articles or reviews – without permission in writing from Josette Reuel.

The characters and events portrayed in this book are fictitious or are used fictitiously. Any similarity to real persons, living or dead, is purely coincidental and not intended by the author.

This ebook is licensed for your personal enjoyment only. This ebook may not be re-sold or given away to other people. If you would like to share this ebook with another person, please purchase an additional copy for each person or use proper retail channels to lend a copy. If you are reading this ebook and did not purchase it, or it was not purchased for your use only, then please return it and purchase your own copy. Thank you for respecting the hard work of this author.

Note: Previously published as part of the "Claiming My Valentine" Anthology on February 14, 2017.

First Edition: September, 2017

ISBN-10: 197762829X
ISBN-13: 978-1977628299

Love Burns is for those readers who enjoy a bit of steam from this side of the bedroom door. A sweet paranormal romance, it takes us on a quick journey with Hy and Brann as they determine what they want from their relationship.

--

Hyacinth Sieress didn't want to get burned by another bad relationship, and for a year she had been doing just fine on her own. Maybe her apartment was less than desired and seeing her ex every time he showed up with work for the agency she worked for wasn't easy, but Hy was determined to be happy. Growing up in foster care, Hy had always been good at putting her best foot forward and making the best of a bad situation, and continued to do so. That was, until she looked up into the deep sea blue eyes of a god.

After meeting Brann Drahgue, Hy's world was turned on its ear. Nightly dreams of the man and working with him all day long... even the prim and proper Hy was bound to break.

Can a dragon claim Hy's heart this Valentine's Day or will love burn her, yet again?

Dedication

To love at first sight and the power of Cupid's arrow when it's not.

Acknowledgments

I have always loved books and writing. This love of words was fostered by my parents, Dean and Cosette. I thank them for their guidance, sacrifice, and belief. To my family – husband, daughter, and son – who support me, love me regardless of my flaws, and always make me laugh, thank you for believing in me and supporting me as I achieve my lifelong goal and dream of sharing my stories.

A huge thanks to all of those on Facebook – authors, readers, family, and friends (those I've met, those I hope to meet one day) – for words of wisdom, for words of joy, and for sharing pieces of your lives with me. So many have helped me to maintain my faith in myself.

A huge thank you to my beta readers, my proofreaders, and editors. You all ROCK! This book wouldn't be where it is without your corrections and suggestions. Reuel's Rebels' Alphas for this book: Ginelle Blanch, Alison Jarvis, Debbie Palmer, Jennifer Alvarez, and Jennifer Cazares. And, a special thank you to all the fans — your support and promotion of my work is invaluable.

Lastly, a special thank you to my PA — Jennifer Rebelle Alvarez — who keeps me on track and provides a sounding board for all of my ideas, stresses, and quirks. Destiny brought us together and I couldn't be more grateful.

Chapter 1

*T*he beginning.

Just over a year ago, Hy's life had imploded when her then fiance and now ex, Tom, was found in flagrante delicto with the next door neighbor. It had taken everything she had to pick up the pieces. There was a time that Hy would have said that she and Tom had a future, and Tom was still pretty adamant that they did, but when she ended the relationship she was more embarrassed than sad. Tom found every reason to bother her — setting up meetings with her boss, having lunch in her town instead of his during the week, and spending time at her favorite hangout…the local bookstore — and he was always trying to talk her into coming back to him. Of course, that was when he wasn't flaunting his newest floozy and telling Hy that she would never find anyone to love her overly ample frame. The one and only excuse he had given for his affair was that Hy wasn't pretty or thin enough to turn him on. The only reason he ever tried to get her back was either because he was on the market or his ego needed the boost. Hy was determined to not give a shit.

Even so, it had been difficult when she packed up and

moved to the small town just over from where she had lived with Tom. Unfortunately, she still saw him, the towns were so close that locals often found themselves in one or the other to supply their needs, but the new town at least gave her a buffer.

Hy didn't try to date or have any real life. She simply went to work, went to the bookstore, the grocery store, and home. As a foster child, she had grown up in many homes and attended many schools, so even today she had few friends. It was a learned mechanism for her, distance herself from others and she wouldn't get hurt. Some how Tom had forced himself past her barriers and she had broken rule one in her survival guide.

Then it happened. Lightning struck. That day six months ago when her gaze lifted from her computer screen and fell into the deep blue eyes of a god.

The sizzle that sped up and down her body was everything Hy had ever read about love at first sight. Her heart raced so fast that it felt like it would burst from her chest. Her mouth went dry and she became a blathering fool.

*

Hyacinth Seirres had just typed the salutation of Mr. Trollmann's letter when the chime alerted her to someone entering the office. She quickly saved the file and gracefully laid her hands on her desktop to show the visitor that she was ready to help them.

Her gaze slid over the edge of her desk and landed on expensive tailored black dress pants, which were not unusual for her boss' clients, but when she roamed her eyes up the dark wool covered legs the journey lasted longer than average, which was unusual when compared to the average men she normally spoke with. The man standing in front of her could not be described as average in any way. He was extremely tall, well built, and dressed immaculately. Continuing her visual journey, she encountered a trim waste and a silky cotton green shirt before finally landing on a masculine face. Hy's perusal of the man only took a few seconds, but when she gazed into the deep ocean depths of the man's eyes, time lost all meaning.

Desire raged through Hy's body and her mouth went dry as flames caressed over her skin.

The twang of a string pulled taunt, didn't pull Hy's gaze away, nor did the ache that bloomed in her chest mere seconds later.

"I'm here to see Mr. Trollmann."

Hyacinth knew that words were escaping the delectable mouth that now attracted her eyes.

The hum of the deep vibrato soothed her aching muscles.

"Miss?" She watched in stunned silence as a hand reached forward and a single finger caressed under her chin. "Are you alright?" He asked as his finger applied pressure and pushed her mouth closed.

"Brann Drahgue!" Mr. Trollmann rushed from his office and clasped the man in one of those classic man hugs. "It's been ages since I've spoken to you, what brings you to my humble office?"

Laughter rang out through the room.

"I wish it was for a visit, but I need your services."

"Come this way then." Hy's boss now wore a grim expression as he waved his friend to precede him into his personal office. "Hyacinth, please hold my calls."

It wasn't until the door clicked shut behind them that Hy felt her brain reboot. That was when several intense emotions surfaced in rapid fire succession.

Mortification. Desire. Lust. Embarrassment. Curiosity. And, a need to be close to the man that had just centered her world. A feeling of rightness that she had never felt before took hold and wrapped her tightly in its comforting embrace.

Her desk phone buzzed and caused Hy to jerk backward, her roller chair tipped precariously on only two of its wheels. It was one of those moments when you swear that time froze as your thoughts went through every possible scenario only to determine that you're doomed.

"Fuck me," Hy yelled as the chair continued its fall and crashed to the floor.

It was that moment that the "god" decided to return as if he had the "godly" ability to know exactly when to enter a room and find a person in the worst possible position. Hyacinth slammed into the padded back of her chair. The force knocked the wind out of her and she struggled to pull air into her lungs. Laying the way she was, her legs stuck up into the air and her skirt floated down to land around her waist and expose her practical cotton underwear.

She prayed that he wouldn't come around the desk, but she obviously was praying to the wrong god, because the man circled her desk in a brisk walk to kneel beside her.

"Are you alright?" He queried as he grasped the arms of her chair and lifted it upright.

The movement was smooth and effortless. She gaped at him as she settled back into the seat part of the office furniture that she had decided to burn as soon as it was feasible.

"Miss, are you injured?"

Shaking her head, Hy responded with a clipped, "No."

"Are you sure? You seem to be struggling to breathe."

"I am, but not from the fall," she mumbled as she pulled herself up and forward in order to stand. "I'm…"

Her voice squeaked like Minnie Mouse and her hand slapped over her mouth as the burn of a blush seeped over her face. The realization that she had spoken out loud and that this man knew exactly what she had meant, had her wishing that she could disappear. Taking an unsteady step, both of Hy's ankles wobbled in her practical heels. Mr. Drahgue must have seen her shaking limbs and thinking it meant she was going to fall again; he reached out and gripped her by the elbow. For such a large man, he maneuvered easily to her side and braced her against his side.

When her god sucked in a breath and inhaled deeply several times, Hyacinth began looking around to see if she had stepped on his toes or bumped him with her extra padding into something uncomfortable.

"*Mi ánde*. Why now?" He mumbled as she felt his chin rest on the top of her head.

"I'm sorry," Hy began as he moved her back to the demon possessed office chair.

"You appear unharmed, so I'll just get back to Marc." His words were clipped and sounded as if he had a god complex to go along with the godly good looks.

She watched him turn on his heel and quickly stride across to Mr. Trollmann's office door. He stopped just as abruptly as he had begun and turned back to look at her.

"Oh, wait, Marc asked me to give you this…" He held out a piece of paper. "…we need you to pick us up some lunch."

He waggled the paper in the air until she got back to her feet once again and walked around her desk to reach him. As soon as her fingers clasped onto the paper, Mr. Drahgue was disappearing behind her boss' closing door.

Hy let out the breath she had been holding and picked up her desk phone to call in the lunch order. While she ordered mu shu pork and egg rolls, her eyes remained glued to the dark cherry wood that shielded the god from her scrutiny.

Chapter 2

*T*he Push — Exes and the mess they bring.

Valentine's Day was fast approaching and Hy was trying her best to ignore the man that continued to torment her each and every day — Brann Drahgue had hired the agency to perform various forms of research and most days found the man in the office assisting. Much of the research centered on family trees and locating current descendants of the original subjects of the searches. Their office boasted two full-time private eyes, three historians with various PhDs and letters after their names, herself, and the owner, Mr. Trollmann. The staff typically kept busy, but since Mr. Drahgue had appeared everyone had been putting in overtime — including herself and Mr. Drahgue.

Hy may not have the training her coworkers had, but she'd learned a lot from them. She could now do much of the basic research, which saved the harder tasks for those that had the knowledge of where and how to look. She typically prided herself on her abilities to lighten the load, but the searches brought to her from their new client appeared unachievable until the genealogists got their eyes on them.

To top it off, she wasn't just professionally discouraged; she was sexually frustrated as well. Inhaling Brann Drahgue's musky scent all day long, it was no wonder she found herself dreaming of his delectable body all night. Hell, forget the frustration, Hy was confused. Up to this point, she'd never had "wet" dreams about anyone. Tom had accused her of being a dud in the sack. He hadn't used he term frigid, but he might as well have for as much as he warmed the cockles of her heart. It only took seeing his hairy, bare ass going up and down on top of another woman in her bed for her to realize that Tom had provided a sense of comfort, not love and not lust. The 'love at first sight' feeling that Brann gave her only cemented the facts regarding her feelings for her ex-fiancee.

The bell chimed as the door opened and Hy looked up hopefully — Brann hadn't arrived yet that morning — only to be disappointed. Think of the devil and he shall come, she thought as a frown curved her lips.

"Yes, Tom, what can I help you with this morning?"

It always took everything she had to be professional with the sleazeball.

"Ah, sweetheart, I'm so glad to find you at your desk." Tom oozed with falseness as he sat on the edge of her desktop.

"Tom, I have a perfectly good chair right over there, as you know since I've told you the last ten times you've been in the office."

The man waved her words off. "That's too far away. I need to speak privately with you." His innuendo was completely understood by the plant in the corner, let alone her co-workers who chose that moment to cross the area as they headed to the break room for coffee.

Hyacinth sighed and counted to ten… twice.

"What about?" She regrettably asked, knowing it was the only way to get rid of him.

"Well, I thought it would be nice if we went out to dinner." Typical Tom, he stated and didn't ask.

"I'm busy."

"I haven't told you when, yet."

"Doesn't matter Tom, Mr. Trollmann needs everyone in the office these days."

"Come on, Cinny, you have to take time to eat."

"Tom, I've asked you not to call me that."

"Fine, Hyacinth. Now, about dinner, I thought we'd go to that…"

"Tom, stop. I told you no. We've hashed this all out. We're done." She punctuated her words by crossing her arms across her chest and sighing with exasperation. "Besides, I've been having to eat at my desk for the past six months."

She watched as several emotions crossed Tom's face before he settled on one. Yep… anger. Why wasn't she surprised? The man couldn't take a hint and was constantly putting her on the spot when she couldn't fight back.

"You might as well be working. It's not like you have

men lined up to ask you to be their valentine." Standing abruptly he leaned across her desk and into her face. "I was only going to help you from spending another holiday alone, Cinny."

Anger began to curdle her stomach when his words sank in, what did he mean "another holiday"?

"There's no sense trying to pretend you have a date, I know you don't."

"Tom, damn it. What are you talking about? For one, you no longer know anything about me, so stop trying to pretend you do. And, two, what do you mean by holiday?"

A deep belly laugh escaped Tom as he bent forward and exaggerated the hilarity of the situation.

"Oh, Cinny, you are just too cute. Valentine's Day is next weekend. But, I guess when you don't date and have no one to send you flowers or chocolate anymore the holiday loses its appeal."

Hy closed her eyes against the pain and anguish that Tom still seemed to be able to pull from her. She refused to pander to the man's ego or to his sick since of humor. That meant she had to stick to her rules which meant no taking his bait.

"Hy, *mi kjerlighet*, here is your tea." Warmth enveloped her with each syllable and wrapped her in the softest of blankets.

For months now, every weekday since that first day — 184 days 5 hours and 23 minutes — not that she was counting, she and the god had been flirting. He'd bring in her favorite tea and she'd bake him cookies. It was nonstop flirting — Brann would find subtle ways to touch her or be near her and Hy would work later than she really needed just so he could walk her to her car at the end of another long day. Even so, it never went farther than harmless flirting back and forth. Hy wanted it to be more, but Brann never made a move to make it anything more than a friendly work relationship.

Warm breath brushed over her face only seconds before soft lips brushed against her own. A nibble followed the simple pressure and Hy's eyelids snapped open to find her obsession leaning down to place the tea on her desk and a kiss across her lips.

Brann's nostrils flared and she could have sworn that something moved in the depths of his stormy blue eyes. The glow from her monitor sparked a glow in his irises that made him appear even more wild and untamed than usual. Denim dragged across her calf as Brann stepped further into her. Oh, yeah, he was wearing the jeans again today. She sighed and Brann groaned.

"*Mi lys*, how you light me up."

Damn, how she loved it when he used those words she didn't understand.

"Excuse me, who is this, Cinny? Cinny, answer me Cinny…"

A growl escaped Brann as he was pulled away from her by the slime bucket that she had hoped was a figment of her imagination. But, soon he had a smile firmly in place and was leaning against her desk with an arm around her waist as she stood watching events unfold.

"I'm her boyfriend, who the hell are you?" Brann asked with an edge of super sweetness.

Hy gaped at both men as the word sunk into her brain and slowly, no matter how hard she tried to prevent it, into her heart.

"Excuse me, I don't think so." Tom laughed.

"Who are you to have any say in my Hyacinth's life?" Brann reached over and pressed lightly under her chin and she felt her lips close together.

"I'm her fiancee," Tom stated with obscene satisfaction.

"The hell you are." Hy couldn't stop the words or the viciousness in which they escaped her lips. This fucking asshat was not trying to ruin a relationship for her. It might be a fake one, but there was no way that he could know that. "You fucking lost the right to know or say anything when you brought a liposuctioned, collagen-enhanced bimbo into my bed."

Hyacinth's body vibrated with the force of her emotions. She was sick and tired of Tom always dropping in and rubbing it in her face that she was alone and unloved. Her friend, Sam, had on multiple occasions told her that she was too polite to Tom, but Hy had always thought it was better to take the high road with the man. On occasion, he had need of the agency's services — that was how they had met in the first place — and she didn't want to take the chance of Mr. Trollmann deciding that she wasn't worth keeping on in her administrative assistant role. If she couldn't handle a few interactions with her ex, then how was he to trust her with his other clients. Like it or not, Tom was a client of the agency and she had learned to bite her lip.

With those sobering thoughts, Hy compelled herself to calm down and speak with Tom in the professional manner she had adopted just for him. Forced cheerfulness was better than trying to find a job in a town that had none available.

Now that she was on her own, the bills were all piling up and waiting for her to pay them. She couldn't afford being unemployed. Splitting up with Tom had already caused her to move into a less than stellar apartment and forego cable or internet to reduce costs. The agency paid well, but living was expensive and Hy refused to put herself in debt just to get by.

With a sigh, she opened her eyes and stared Tom down. She might have to be polite, but she was damn well going to give him some indication of her anger at his words.

"Tom, you and I haven't been together for a year. Please don't tell people that we're together?"

"Cinny, if you'd stop being stubborn we could finish the plans for the wedding." Tom's voice rang with condescension and hubris as he puffed out his chest.

"Tom…"

"No, wait, Hyacinth." Brann grasped her hand and waited for her to give him permission to speak.

All she could do was stare at him dumbfounded. Having spent more time than she liked to remember letting Tom bully her into doing what he wanted, Hy wasn't used to having someone ask her permission. A simple nod of her head in the affirmative was all she was able to get out, as once again Brann pressed his fingers against her chin. Jaw dropping was becoming an embarrassing occurrence around this man.

"You're going to swallow flies if you keep that up, *mi ánde*," he whispered into her ear on an airy chuckle just before turning a harsh glare on Tom.

"Hyacinth may be too polite to tell you this, but I'm not. You're being an ass and need to leave."

"Brann, no!" Hy yelled in horror.

She could see her job slipping through her fingers.

"He's quite right, Hyacinth. I won't let clients harass my staff. No amount of business is worth you putting up with this shit." Mr. Trollmann advanced and open the door for Tom to leave.

She had never discussed her personal life with her boss for fear that he would let her go. It would have been the prudent thing. Hy didn't want to be the reason for the loss in business that would impact her co-workers getting paid.

"You should have come to me about this, Hyacinth." The man actually winked at her before turning to Tom. "Now Mr. Barnes, if your company has need of my agencies services I'd prefer for them to send someone else to the office in the future. You are no longer welcome, good day, sir."

Brann's arm tightened around her waist as he slid her into his side. The feeling the movement elicited inside her could only be described as 'coming home.' In this man's embrace, she felt safe for the first time in… well… ever.

As a child raised in foster care since she was three years old, Hy had lived in her fair share of shitty environments. Thankfully, in eighth grade the state had placed her with the James'. They were an older couple who had lost their only son after he enlisted in the service at eighteen. His death hadn't broken the couple; instead, it had opened their hearts to many others. Upon their death a few years back, the kindly couple had helped over five hundred kids weather the system. A few like Hy had stayed for years, but others had been with them for only a few days, weeks, or months before their home situations were straightened out and they were able to go home. But, each of those children had been assured that they had a permanent safe place if they ever needed it. After the horrific accident that had claimed the couple on impact, all five hundred plus of those children had attended the funeral. Hy hadn't understood the extent of the couple's generosity until the families stood up and gave thanks to the couple that had helped them save themselves and their family. From paying for groceries to helping them check into rehab or finding a house, the couple had done more than offer their home to the children, they had made the child's entire family part of their own.

Since the James' deaths, Hy had felt adrift and alone. Not even her friendship with Sam or her relationships with her co-workers had filled the void left by the couple that had shown her what love was. No one, that was, until Brann Drahgue.

"Now, now, *mi kjérlighet*. No tears," he said as he softly wiped them away with his fingers. "That, *drittsikk*, isn't worth them."

Hy shook her head, but couldn't open her mouth to explain that the tears weren't due to Tom, but due to Brann himself.

"Hyacinth, I want you to take the rest of the day off. I can tell that Mr. Barnes has you stressed. Take some time for yourself and return tomorrow with the knowledge that we won't allow him to harass you any longer." Mr. Trollmann gave her an affectionate pat on the arm before disappearing back into his office.

"Marc is correct, *mi lys*, you should take the afternoon."

"I'm alright Mr. Drahgue. Thank you for standing up to Tom, but I'm used to dealing with him."

Hyacinth swore that a rumble, something like a growl, came from Brann.

He slid his fingers over her face and scooped up the hair that had fallen down into her eyes. The caress of his fingers over her ears as he tucked the strands out of the way sent a shiver down her spine. Hy wasn't sure if it was fear or excitement that caused the goosebumps on her arms and the electrical shocks throughout her system, but she was beginning to realize that she was ready to find out.

"You are not alone and do not need to stand up to that *drittsikk*."

"That might be true, but I can all the same." When his lips formed a new syllable, she shushed him with her fingers pressed against those plushly kissable lips.

"Thank you," she said as she moved to gather her things. "I think an afternoon off is exactly what I need."

Not because of Tom, but to sort out her feelings regarding the ruggedly handsome man standing beside her desk.

Chapter 3

*T*he Plan — Operation Cupid's Arrow.

A short time later Hy found herself sipping her favorite herbal tea as she waited for Sam to have a moment free from the customers at the Daily Vice. The bookstore was a cross between a bookstore and coffee shop that also catered to those searching for a music or snack fix. To die for snacks comprised of a mix of sweets that always left Hy drooling. Today was the first time that she wasn't tempted by the pastries and candies created by the stores two full-time chefs. Her friend had taken every step to make sure her dream of the perfect meeting place for those seeking to commune with their muse came to life. Even the decorations were for sale on consignment from local artists.

"So why aren't you at work? I love having ya, but I don't ever remember you missing a day of school, let alone work." Hy slowly raised her eyes to look into Sam's concerned expression.

"Tom showed up at work today." She tilted her cup to her lips, taking a deep sip of the spicy brew as she sought out the right words to explain her current situation.

Sam was one of the sweetest people she knew, but the girl also had a healthy helping of spunk that kept her from holding her tongue when she felt strongly enough about something. This time was no different.

"That Cock-Sucking-Belly-Crawler, what the fuck was he doing there, Hy?"

Swallowing the warm liquid, Hy braced herself for Sam's next response.

"He wanted me to go to dinner…"

"Hell no, Hy. Please tell me you're not that stupid?"

"If you'd let me finish I would." Hy grinned at her friend to take the sting out of her words.

She loved Sam, but at times she wished her friend showed a bit more restraint when voicing her thoughts. Several customers were currently looking over their books and pastries at them and the public scrutiny was something that Hy had never been able to handle. Sam must have noticed the tension coming from her, because she turned to her customers and waved her hands at them.

"Sorry, Hy. How about we go to my office? The girls can handle things out here."

Without waiting for an answer Sam was on the move. She stopped briefly to yell at her employees to watch the front and continued on to her office without missing a step. Hy scrambled to keep up with her friend and quietly closed the door once she entered the small office where Sam conducted the less fun part of her business: bookkeeping, placing orders, and the like.

The storekeeper had papers scattered everywhere and shuffled them quickly around so that the chair was clear for Hy to sit. For a brief second, Hy thought of leaving her friend to her own troubles, because she knew something was going on… Sam was not one to be disorganized. Everything was sorted and labeled with precision, so to find a mess of paperwork was telling of Hy's friend's own mind and emotions.

"Don't even think of deflecting." Sam wagged a finger at her. "Now, sit and spill. What the hell happened that you are taking time off of work?"

Moving around so much in her younger years, Hy never had a chance to make any deep connections with the other children, but when she moved in with the James' Sam had already been with the couple for a few months. Both girls were orphans that had gotten lost in the systems trail of red tape. But, where Hy became introverted and fell back on manners to get by in the world. Sam had learned to be more brash. Her friend wasn't outward going per say, she barricaded her heart from pretty much everyone and everything, but she could hold her own in a social situation. Unlike Hy, who closed down and clammed up when she was put on the spot. Thankfully for both girls, the James' had provided them an outlet for their energy and a way to pull them from their shells - they had introduced the girls to music, art, and books. Sam had opened her business as an homage to the couple and to provide a place for kids like they were — kids that needed a place to hang out and to absorb the arts.

"I'm waiting, Hy, and I don't have all afternoon. Unlike you, I have work to do… several shipments are on their way as we speak."

"I know Sam, I just don't know where to begin." Hy squirmed in the straight back chair. "You know I'm not comfortable talking about myself."

"Hy, I'm your best friend, just spit it the hell out."

"Okay, okay… remember how I told you about Mr. Drahgue?"

"You mean Mr. Hunky-Client," Sam said while making all kinds of facial expressions to get the underlying message of her words across.

Shaking her head at her friend Hy continued, "Since I know that's what *you* call him, why, yes. Mr. Drahgue and I have been spending a lot of time together. I'm guessing a lot more time than I led you to believe. We sort of… well, you know, we… well…"

"Just say it, Hy, geesh!"

"We flirt. A lot." Hy felt the burn as the blush sped across her face.

Even after all of their years of friendship, Hy still didn't feel comfortable discussing anything remotely sexual with her friend.

Sam jumped up from her chair and pulled a box over

in front of Hy's chair. Sitting on the box, Sam took her hands and squeezed them tight in reassurance.

"I'm sorry, Hy. It's been a rough few weeks, little sleep and lots of paperwork for the shop. I shouldn't take that out on you. And, before you say it, no I haven't told you about what is going on. I'm not ready to share any of it and may never be. Which makes me a hypocrite, I know, but you're my friend and I can tell that you need to talk."

The pathetic look that Sam gave her brought forth a weak laugh. Bending forward, Hy hugged her friend before sitting back to continue.

"Yes, I do need to talk, and don't think you're getting off that easy, we'll get back to you soon. But, for now… I'm really confused and I don't know what to think about Mr. Drahgue. I've done everything possible to force his hand to get him to admit to some sort of feelings. I mean some of the things he says and does… I just don't see someone with platonic feelings acting the way he does. But, it's almost as if he shuts down when things get too personal. I'm the first to admit that I'm clueless when it comes to relationships. Tom was my one and only and he had made all of the moves."

Hyacinth ran out of air and stopped to stunned silence. Sam looked at her like she had two heads for several long minutes.

"Wow. You have feelings for him, don't you?"

"No…" Sam gave her a look of disbelief and Hy knew she couldn't deny what she had been lying to herself about for weeks. "Yes… well, maybe. I've never felt this way. He makes me feel all tingly and happy and breathless and dizzy…" A quick breath was all she allowed herself to go on. "Other than you and the James' I've never felt love, at least not that I can remember. Being in the system since three has left me with very little to go on when it comes to feelings."

Sam shook her head in understanding and motioned for her to continue.

"I think this could be love. I look forward to working with him each day and feel sad if he doesn't show up. Then there are the dreams and what he did for me today. It's frustrating and confusing. And, I need my best friend to help me sort this out."

Sam's hand flew up to press her palm out in the air. "Stop right there. What dreams? And, after you explain them then you can tell me about today. You can't just throw something like that out there and not explain, Hy. Especially if you want me to help you."

Hyacinth's shoulders dropped and she exhaled loudly.

"I know," she whispered. "I just don't know if I can. Those dreams are really personal."

Hy cleared her throat and looked at Sam. When her friend simply stared her down, Hy continued. "You know… they're intimate."

The red in her cheeks deepened again and Hy felt flushed with embarrassment.

"For fuck's sake, Hy, you're a grown woman. Wet dreams are normal. Especially when you've been celibate for a year."

"Damn it, Sam. I'm not comfortable with this. It's difficult to talk about. Give me some slack. You knew what I meant anyhow. But, yes, I've had wet dreams of Brann since the first day we met and his flirting with me hasn't made it any easier. Then today he stood up to Tom for me. He told Tom that we were dating and then he and Mr. Trollmann kicked Tom out of the office. To top everything off, Mr. Trollmann told me to take the afternoon off and reprimanded me for not telling him about Tom sooner."

"Oh, wow. I think that's the most open and honest you've ever been."

Hy looked up from her clenched hands to find Sam smirking at her. She cuffed her friend's arm and chuckled.

"Screw you too, Sam."

"Seriously, Hy, I told you that you should have told Mr. Trollmann about Tom ages ago. I'm not surprised that your boss told you the same thing. As for your *dream* man, Brann. Damn, that's a fine name. You do realize that's the first time you've called him by his given name? He was always Mr. Drahgue before this."

Sam sat back on the box and leaned against her desk. Her fingers drummed the cardboard that had begun to cave under her weight as she closed her eyes to think. This was her friend's MO, she would pull the information from you and then leaned her head back and ran through scenarios in her own mind before making any suggestions.

"Maybe, maybe it will work. Hmm…"

Hy was getting impatient as her friend mumbled to herself. She knew what she wanted and she wanted to force Brann to make his true feelings known. The addition of making Tom eat all of his words about how unlovable she was, would be a very enjoyable bonus of getting the man she wanted.

Hyacinth stood and walked over to the wall opposite the door. She assessed her image in the full-length mirror that hung there. Her first reaction was to tell herself all of the negative things — her brown hair and her skin tone, neither tan or pale, were totally average. She was average height as well. Unfortunately, a bit heavier than she would like, she really wasn't obese nor stick thin. Her negative thoughts always led to her conclusion that she was forgettable. Hell, for all she knew her own parents had forgotten her — no, she wouldn't go there. Hy shoved the thought deep in the box that she locked away the negative things she didn't want to remember. It didn't matter to her, because to her, her birth parents were dead or as good as in her mind. That was enough. It was enough that she had found a loving couple her last four years before turning eighteen and a friend that became her family.

Shaking off thoughts she didn't want to entertain, Hy compelled herself to look in the mirror with new eyes. It was true that in many respects she was average, but Hy wouldn't call herself plain. She had good bone structure and her eyes were mesmerizing. Many people had commented on her eyes — a deep gray that in many cases looked almost black, flecks of lighter gray gave them the appearance of stars across a night sky. The warm golden ring around her pupil contradicted the coolness of the other colors. On more than one occasion Sam and the James' had joked that her eyes glowed when she became overly passionate about something, but she hadn't ever seen what they had and had pushed it to the side as a weird reflection of light off the gold ring. However, now, thinking about Brann, she could almost see an effervescence quality due to the gold and gray contrast. She blinked and jumped as she turned around thinking Sam had moved, when she realized that her friend was still deep in thought, her focus returned to the mirror. She struggled to keep her eyelids from blinking as she watched for what she'd seen reflected in the mirror just seconds before.

There! There it was. Something moved in the dark depths of her reflected eyes that were beginning to water. Stinging pain caused her to finally blink and keep them closed for several moments. She couldn't follow the movements in her own eyes; most likely the light was playing off of the shiny glass surface. She sighed and collapsed back onto the hard chair.

The one thing that she hated about asking Sam for advice was the waiting. She always felt like she was going mad by the time her friend decided to speak. This time, however, she welcomed the time to think on her own. She wanted Brann, that was true. She wouldn't deny her feelings, but she was going to be honest with herself. The idea that Brann could have similar feelings for her were a million to one. What was she actually wanting her friend to tell her? A lie? A truth? Something in between? *Gah!* Hy huffed to herself.

"OPERATION CUPID'S ARROW!" Sam jumped up as the words came out at top volume.

Hyacinth jerked in her chair, causing it to tip backward precariously on only two of the four legs. She flung her arms out frantically searching for something to pull herself forward, when she felt herself slap skin. When the chair settled and Hy could breathe again, Sam looked at her with concern. Hy's fingers were still tightly clenched onto her friend's arms.

"Sorry, you startled me," she mumbled as she forced the muscles to release so she could detach from Sam. "Now, what was that you were yelling about Cupid's arrow?"

Sam laughed and bounced up and down on the box that was never going to be square again. "Operation Cupid's Arrow! We're going to get you your man."

Sam's enthusiasm was contagious and Hy couldn't hold back the giggles that wanted to escape. "Okay. How is this operation going to work?"

Hy's friend spent a bit too much time watching TV shows and reading obviously. They had never named their plans of action before, but somehow it felt oddly appropriate this time.

"Okay, so, you said that Brann claimed to be your boyfriend, Yes?" Hy nodded in response and waited. "Well, Valentine's Day is fast approaching and Tom has made an ass of himself in front of the man, I don't think it will be too hard to convince Brann that Tom is still harassing you about that date."

"All right, but what good is that going to do?"

"Well, that's where I come in... I'm going to teach

you how to seduce him."

"What?!" Hy squeaked through her tightening throat.

"Yes, this will work. All you have to do right now is get him to agree to the date. Simply, tell him that a public outing with another man will force Tom to acknowledge that it's over. Tom is very conscious of his reputation and he wouldn't want to lose face in front of his friends and colleagues by chasing after an already attached woman. It's simplicity at its best."

"Sam, you forget I'm a horrible liar and even worse at seduction."

"Don't worry." Her friend jumped up and pulled open the office door. "I'm going to teach you. We'll start tonight while you help me accept the deliveries and restock the store."

Cocking her head at Sam, Hy pursed her lips and grunted.

"Don't you dare say I planned this. I was not going to ask you to help me. Nope. I'm doing this all out of kindness."

When Hy kept giving Sam the "yeah, right" face, her friend busted out into raucous fits of laughter.

"Just get your butt off that chair and we'll begin your lessons with how to walk."

Hyacinth was afraid that the whole plan was going to backfire spectacularly and she'd have to find a way to place herself into a witness protection program. There had to be a crime somewhere that she could witness and go to court to testify about, right?

"Not like that, Hy, you have to sway your hips more."

Oh, fuck. It was going to be a long night.

Chapter 4

*T*he Execution - By guillotine or sexy god?

"Simone…" Austin stroked his fingers down the arm that had remained at her side. "I'm sorry for laughing. It was stupid and I shouldn't have." Thirty-six grueling hours and a second day off of work had finally culminated into Sam announcing that she was ready. Lack of sleep and several tear jerker movies later, Hy walked into work with red puffy eyes, dark circles, and a plan.

Sam had Hy go into work late, and she could swear that she felt a panic attack coming on. What the hell had she been thinking? Why in the world would she listen to Sam and this crazy plan? Hyacinth had never missed a day of work, let alone two and coming in late had never been acceptable either. If Sam caused her to lose her job, she'd make the woman allow her to move into Sam's apartment and support her until she found a new one.

Clutching a huge box of tissues to her chest, Hy balanced a tray full of extremely full and steaming cardboard coffee cups in her other hand. While pushing the door open with her ass per Sam's directions. Right on cue she dropped the box of tissues and bent over to pick them up while propping the door open with her body. A moan sounded from behind her as a strong hand relieved her of the coffee. Hy deeply inhaled the outside air, stepped into the office, and promptly ran into a hard chest. Brann grabbed her around the waist with the hand not holding the coffees. His long fingers caressed along her lower back, causing a shiver to race down Hy's spine. Her body trembled as she compelled her to gaze up at Brann's face.

"*Mi lys!*" Brann pulled Hy over to her desk and relieved them both of their burdens. He gripped her upper arms with more force than he most likely realized — Hy could already feel bruises forming — as he searched her face for answers. Hy wondered what the questions were as she watched his expression change from one of concern to rage and back again. Over the months Hy felt she had gotten a good reading on the man and he was definitely angry, but not at her.

"What happened, *mi kjerlighet?*"

Brann's masculine fingers ran across Hy's features. The roughness of the pads a testament to the strong man that stood before her. Even with such strength, she was more impressed with the compassion he showed towards her rough and weary appearance.

"Tell me, Hyacinth, who upset you?" His voice vibrated with a deepness she had never heard from him before.

She almost feared to tell him it was Tom. Brann had always been kind to her, but the quality of his voice had her fearing that he would go off after whoever had hurt her. A split second passed before she internally smacked herself. She wouldn't deny the appeal of Tom being put into his place by Brann, but it wouldn't be right. Because, for once, Tom really hadn't done anything. She bit her lip to remind herself of the plan.

"Don't worry about me, Mr. Drahgue. I'm fine. I'll be able to get some of the legwork done on those documents you wanted to track down. I'm so sorry about not being here yesterday. I know how important this work is to you." Hy sniffed and reached for a tissue for good measure.

Her friend had been adamant that Hy shows both weakness and strength. Sam had insisted, "No friend of mine is going to let a man think she's a doormat. In need of rescue, but still strong enough to stand on her own two feet. It's a fine line for this to work, Hy."

It didn't matter that they wanted him to worry about her. Brann would offer his assistance if he was a gentleman. If he didn't, Sam believed it meant that he wasn't worth Hy's concern.

"*Faen ditte*! I'm not worried about those damn papers right now. The others can do the research. Right now, I want you to tell me why the hell you look like you've been crying all night."

Hyacinth fell into Brann's chest and proceeded to pretend-sob into the man's shirt.

"There, there, *mi kjerlighet*. You are safe. You're with those that care."

"What's going on?" Hy heard Mr. Trollmann ask from the direction of his door.

"I don't know, but she looks like she's been up crying all night."

"I bet it was that Tom Barnes. I knew he was slime, but I didn't know she was dating him until she moved in with him. It wasn't until she updated her address that I even knew they had split."

Brann's chest once again rumbled with an aggressive growl.

"Brann, watch your emotions." Mr. Trollmann's voice came from beside her.

Her boss' statement was only a blip of confusion before she was distracted by Brann pulling her away from him.

"Was it him, *mi ánde*? Did he bother after we told him to leave you alone?"

Brann's eyes were closed when she finally looked up and Hy worried that he'd break his jaw with how tightly clenched together his teeth were.

"I appreciate your and Mr. Trollmann's concern, but this is my mess to clean up."

"Damn it, Hyacinth, his name is Marc and mine is Brann. I don't want to step on your modern woman's toes, but females should be protected by their male family members. You are such a small thing… No match for a man's size."

Hyacinth bristled at his words. She had been taking care of herself since she was three years old and would continue to do so until her last breath. She was drawn to Brann, but that didn't mean she was looking to be anyone's china doll sat up on a shelf or wrapped in bubble wrap. Hy might prefer to be demure and polite, but it didn't mean she was weak.

"Now you hear me, Mr. Drahgue, I haven't had male relatives for long enough to call bullshit on that statement. I might prefer to be polite, but it doesn't mean I don't have a backbone." Poking her finger sharply into his chest to punctuate her statements, Hy was not calmed by his response.

With a chuckle Brann, pulled her into his arms. Hy struggled to place distance between them, but the man was a solid mass of muscles and bone. Mr. Trollmann's chuckle fired her up even more.

"Of course, *mi lys*, I apologize. I was just trying to say that sometimes you need to lean on the strength of others. Marc and I want to help you, please let us. Tell us what happened to upset you so, I was worried when you didn't show up for work yesterday. Especially when Marc told me it was so unlike you."

Hy tilted her head backward and with her eyes closed she took several deep breaths. She needed to remember Operation Cupid's Arrow. No way was she going to allow a moment of agitation to waste a day and a half of forced instruction from Sam. Having your best friend teach you about seduction was not comfortable in the slightest, and she was determined to make the outcome worth the thirty-six hours of embarrassment.

"Please, Hyacinth. Let us help?" Mr. Trollmann added from off to her right.

"Fine. Tom showed up and insisted that I paid you both off…" She paused to allow them to infer what she meant. "Anyway, he yelled, made threats, and kept trying to get me to agree to dinner with him on Valentine's Day. When I told him I couldn't because of the date with Mr. Drahg…" Hy saw his mouth begin to form the chastisement and corrected herself before he could. "I mean the date with Brann. He laughed at me and accused me again of paying for a gigolo. He said there was no way someone like Brann could be interested in someone like me and the sooner I accepted that and came back to him, the better it would be for both of us. I don't know what would have happened if Sam hadn't shown up with a friend of hers and kicked him out. Sadly, in this instance, you were correct, Brann. Being a woman alone, I had no protection from him."

The lies rolled off of her tongue easier than she had imagined. It wasn't difficult to say these things about Tom because he had said all of those things and more throughout their relationship and during the year since. Hy still couldn't fathom why he wouldn't let her go, why was she so important to him when he couldn't even keep his dick in his pants for her?

"Oh, *mi kjerlighet.*" Brann caressed along her jaw line. "The timing is so off right now."

"When it comes to Fate, my friend, you don't get to choose the time." Mr. Trollmann patted Brann's shoulder before taking a seat on the edge of Hy's desk.

It wasn't the first time that the two men had shared strange phrases with one another and Hy wasn't given a chance to think too much about this one regarding fate.

Mr. Trollmann tapped his fingers against the wood where he braced himself on the desk. A wicked smile soon covered the typically calm and calculated man's face.

"The only thing the two of you can do is to actually go out on that date."

Hy's jaw dropped as she realized that she wasn't going to have to find a way to make the suggestion herself. Brann's jaw dropped and he stared gape-mouthed at his friend. Mr. Trollmann continued to grin as he crossed his arms and nodded his head in affirmation of things being settled.

"Yes, that is exactly what you must do. You'll need to take her to a spot, or maybe several, where there is a chance of Hyacinth being seen by Tom and all of his friends. What do you think, Hyacinth, any suggestions? You know Mr. Barnes the best of all of us."

For a change, Hy reached over and pressed under Brawn's stubble covered chin to close his mouth as she closed her own.

"Mr. Trollmann that is a nice offer on Brann's behalf…"

"Marc, Hyacinth. After all of these years working for me, call me Marc for the gods' sake."

She gave the man a shy smile. "Marc, as I said it's a nice offer, but I'm sure Brann has a date already set up with someone else."

"The hell I do," Brann snapped before closing his lips over an inhuman growl.

Hy wasn't sure why this man made so many strange noises, but she'd be lying if she didn't admit to how sexy she found them.

Brann struggled with himself for awhile, then he turned to Hyacinth and took her hands in his own.

"Hyacinth Seiress, would you do me the honor of accompanying me out to dinner this upcoming Tuesday."

It seemed strange to Hyacinth, the formality in which he phrased his request and the look of uncertainty that sat on his brow. Everything began to have a surreal feel and Hy wondered if she might be dreaming. A quick pinch to the inside of her wrist -- the only part that her fingers could reach from the grip that Brann had on her wrists -- was inconclusive, she didn't wake, but seriously did pain in a dream really wake you up? Hy never remembered her dreams, nothing solid anyhow, so she had no clue if the old wives' tale was accurate or not.

"Hyacinth, *mi ánde*, I understand if you don't…"

"Oh, no wait. No, no…" Brann's faced collapsed and Hy realized her mistake. "No, I mean yes. Yes, I will go to dinner with you, Brann Drahgue."

"Good. Then it's settled. I'll leave the two of you to your plans." As Marc smiled -- Hy didn't think she would ever get used to thinking of him that way -- fear flashed through her. Did he know about the plan that Sam and she had devised?

"Yes, Hyacinth, Marc made a good point that you would know the best date spots for us to visit."

Relief shot through her as she realized what Marc had meant by "plans."

"Yes," she replied. "Tom loves Sansotta's Fine Italian on route 7 And he usually goes out to the Rouge Club a block or so down. Either of those would be good outings to be seen by Tom."

"Good, I'll pick you up at seven." Brann squeezed her hands before letting them drop to her side.

"Okay, which one did you want to go to? I'll call and get us squared away. I know people at both and can make sure that we can get in. Valentine's Day is pretty busy." Picking up a pen she spun her notepad and was poised to take down Brann's choice.

"We'll go to both. I want to make sure that *drittsikk* understands to whom you belong." Brann's face hardened until his eyes fell back to Hy's face. "Oh, I meant that you belonged to yourself, Hyacinth."

Hy's heart dropped as he explained the wording. The man had been correct the first time, she belonged to him. Even if he never accepted her, Hy had a suspicion that a part of her would always long for this man.

"Yes. Both sounds great, I'll make the arrangements and expect to meet you here at seven."

"Arrangements are fine, but I'll pick you up at your house, *mi lys*."

"Alright, sounds good. I'll just make the calls and then we can meet in the conference room, so I can catch up on where we're at with your ancestry searches."

Hyacinth felt flushed and dizzy as Brann leaned in and pressed his lips against the corner of her own.

"Until then, *mi ánde*."

Chapter 5

*T*he Valentine's Day date.

Just under a week had passed since Brann had agreed to their date. Work had been nerve wracking as she waited for him to arrive and tell her that he couldn't take her out after all, that his girlfriend was in town and wanted to spend the holiday with him. The guillotine never fell.

Instead, Brann arrived each morning with a smile, her favorite herbal tea from Daily Vice, and those softly spoken phrases that made her skin buzz and her heart warm. He constantly called for her help with things and they discussed everything from favorite movies, any of the Marvel Universe for her and The Lord of the Rings for him, to favorite books.

Playful arguments ensued as Brann told her that the Hulk would decimate Thor in a fair fight. Hy hit him back with Dr. Who being the first true pioneer of sci-fi television while Brann backed Star Trek. Hy had laughed more each day than she could ever remember laughing her entire life.

Brann just seemed to get her need for solitude when

she was working, but also seemed to instinctively know when she needed to take a break. He got her subtle nuances and never degraded the things she enjoyed like sci-fi and fantasy movies or the romance novels she'd piled on her nightstand. He contrasted so brightly against her one relationship with a man — with Tom — that Hy realized that she had never truly had a relationship with her ex. There had been no give and take, no acceptance of her by him, no laughter, or love if she was honest.

The days had been amazing, but today — Valentine's Day — not so much. Hyacinth should be on cloud nine, but instead, she was fighting a virus that had attacked her system from one of the sites she had searched for data on a few of the older individuals. Medieval records were sparse and typically difficult to decipher. She had made it through so much of the data and was determined not to lose it to the computer worm that seemed to be devouring everything.

Murphy had nothing on Hy as the day wore on with no resolution. While the time of her date inched closer, Hyacinth debated canceling because she knew that she needed to make up for all of the lost data. She didn't have all of the details on what the data was for but knew that Brann was on a deadline.

But for the first time in her life, she wanted to be selfish. She wanted to go on this date. Besides, she rationalized, Brann hadn't seemed overly concerned. She pushed away the doubts and the knowledge that the last the man had known they were working to retrieve the data.

She'd worry about work tomorrow. Tonight she was going to take for herself.

Pounding echoed through her apartment and Hy glanced quickly into the mirror before rushing out of the bathroom. She wasn't one for a bunch of makeup and primping, but per Sam's insistence she'd done up her eyes and slid into the silky green dress that clung in all of the right places.

As she turned the deadbolt the knocking ceased. Swinging the door open, her smile dropped as she took in Sam's look of disapproval.

"Did you even look through the peephole? What if I had been Tom?" Sam's words were flying a mile a minute while she pushed past Hy. "I knew you couldn't be trusted. I told you to apply that lipstick and put on some bling."

Sam tossed a pink plastic bag to the sofa as she pulled a tube of lipstick from her pocket.

"Come here and pucker up." Sam waggled her eyebrows and grinned.

When Hy didn't move immediately she tapped her foot in impatience.

"Your date will be here soon, come on Hy, you said you'd follow my instructions."

"Fine. But, I can put on my own damn lipstick." Hy reached out for the tube of lip color Sam had in her hand. "It's just going to wear off anyhow."

"That's why you carry it in your clutch and reapply often." Sam sighed as she handed the lipstick over and then reached for the bag on the sofa. "By the way, here's a clutch I picked up."

Hy looked down at the glittery green clutch that matched her dress perfectly.

"I knew it was perfect. Now turn around." She motioned with her hand and as Hy looked into her friend's eyes she knew she'd better shut up and do as told.

Sam had a fanatical gleam in her eyes that told Hy she wasn't going to be swayed. Hy turned and felt Sam's arms go around her neck. Sam was a few inches shorter and when Hy felt the cold touch of metal on her bare neck she bent her knees to make things easier on her friend.

Just as Sam patted her back with a muffled "all done," a crisp knock sounded at the door.

Hy's chest tightened at the knowledge of Brann's presence on the other side of the door. She wasn't sure why, but she knew in her gut that the man stood waiting on her just the other side of the metal door.

Sam rushed forward and stuck her eye up to the peephole. She turned back to Hy fanning herself and mouthed "It's him." Then her friend grasped the knob and pulled the door open.

"Hello, handsome, Hy is just grabbing her wrap."

Hy felt her chest tighten and the air vibrated in her chest as she exhaled. A twinge of jealousy shot through her and she stumbled as a gravelly growl escaped her lips. Thankfully, Sam was busy talking to Brann and hadn't invited the man in, so neither saw her as she struggled for breath and understanding of her own actions.

She grabbed the wool wrap from the sofa arm and forced herself to walk to the door. As she passed the mirror on the wall leading to the door, she noticed the dragon pendant the Sam had placed around her neck. The silver chain hung just low enough for the rearing green jeweled dragon to fall in the hollow of her throat. It was gorgeous and she would have to thank her friend -- and pay her back for the necklace and matching clutch. Her shock over the pendant passing Hy gave herself a quick once over, starting at the strappy heels on her feet, her bare calf, and up the billowy green skirt of her dress, which flared out from just under her breasts. She loved the lace sleeves that covered her arms all the way to just past her wrists. The dress was a one in a million find and had been specially designed for a customer of the local bridal shop. When the customer didn't pick it up, the dress was moved to the clearance rack. It fit Hy perfect and she couldn't help but think that fate was on her side.

Relief washed over her as she took in the subtle shade of the lipstick that Sam had bullied her into wearing. Her friend had been right, the deeper red hue and shine the lipstick added to her lips made them even more kissable if she said so herself. A quick double check of her eyes caused Hy to stumble once more, the slight glow effect seemed to swirl around her iris. Hyacinth saw something move in the depths of her own eyes. A presence showed itself and she sucked in a breath of shock.

"*Mi ánde*, you are breathtaking." Brann's voice broke through her own thoughts and she looked up into eyes the same deep blue of the ocean depths.

Silver flecks and a silver ring seemed to glow in those God-like eyes the same way that Hy had noticed her own doing in her reflection. Seeing the similar enhancement, Hy rationalized what she saw as a side effect of the eyeliner she had used. She never used the stuff, so maybe some had gotten into her eyes and was causing this distortion of light and motion. Yes, she thought, that is exactly what it had to be.

Brann reached out and clasped onto her fingers, lifting her hand to his lips he laid a soft kiss against her skin. A zap of awareness accompanied the brush of his lips and Hy felt her heart rate pick up speed.

"Your beauty is all I see, *mi lys*. I am honored that you accepted my request for dinner tonight, Hyacinth Seiress. Shall we go?" Brann offered his arm and Hy accepted on autopilot she simply stared at the man as he led her outside to his truck.

Hyacinth barely registered Sam's yelled goodbye, "Have a good time you two… and don't do anything I wouldn't do." Her friend's laughter cut off with the closing of the door.

She remained in a fog until Brann parked in front of Sansotta's. The restaurant wasn't huge, just a small mom and pop type of location tucked away into a strip of brick businesses on the edge of the business district. Brann circled the hood of the truck and offered his arm to assist her out of the truck once he had her door open. Stepping lightly to the ground with a grace that she never realized she had, she linked her arm into Brann's for him to escort her into the restaurant.

Hy was mesmerized by everything around her. She had never noticed the ethereal beauty created by the twinkle lights that were draped along the ceilings of the restaurant. The classic layout of white cloth covered tables, the black lacquered furniture, and variation of reds on the walls lent a feeling of tradition. Not once had the place felt so steeped in the promise of a future filled with love as it did this night.

Brann did everything just right. He Helped her unwrap herself from her wrap, pulled out the chair for her to sit, and offered to allow her to pick the wine. He didn't even blink an eye when she ordered her favorite Moscato — for most, the sweetness of it was more appropriate to dessert, but Hy liked what she liked, and when you didn't drink much alcohol sweet and fruity were better on the palate.

"So, *mi kjerlighet*, what shall we talk about?"

"How about you tell me something about your past, your family, where you grew up… you know that type of stuff?"

"Nah, you wouldn't be interested in any of that."

"Of course I would."

Brann chuckled.

"We moved around a lot until about a year ago. My parents both passed away within a few months of each other."

"Oh, I'm sorry, Brann. I lost my parents when I was three. I don't even remember them. I think it makes it easier to deal with their loss — I don't have any memories to make me happy or sad."

"Oh, *mi lys*. That had to be difficult, but you had your

family."

"No, I didn't. I was found by a traveler with a bag of clothes, my birth certificate, and not much else. When the state checked into my background they determined that the birth certificate was falsified. They could find no one to connect to me. They chose to keep the name and birth date from the certificate, but otherwise, I don't even know what else was on the paper. It was destroyed or lost somewhere along the way as I jumped from one home to another."

Brann reached across the table and squeezed her fingers. "No, I don't think that was easier at all, Hyacinth." He looked like he wanted to say something more, but kept his lips firmly closed.

"Brann, you can ask me anything you want." She returned the squeeze to his fingers that remained wrapped around her hand.

"It's just… you know nothing about your family, who you are, where you're from?"

It was strange that he focused on her lack of a family connection, most people seemed more fixated on the foster homes and how she had never been adopted.

"No, but it's no bother, the James'— that's the couple that took care of Sam and me all through high school — they were great and now I have Sam."

"But, Hyacinth, the connection to your ancestry and who your people are… I couldn't imagine living without that."

"Then tell me about yours, prove to me that I missed

out on something. Sam and I... neither one of us had any family, we grew up hopping from one foster home to another. Put into the system at an age where we were too old for adoption and too young to be tolerable, no one wanted to keep us for very long. Believe it or not, Sam and I were both a bit of a handful when we were younger." Hy grinned across the table and concentrated on the shadows created by the flickering candlelight from the table's centerpiece.

Before Brann could speak, the waiter returned with their wine and took their food order. It was no surprise that Brann went for the steak fillet. What was surprising was when he asked for a double order, including double the vegetables. She couldn't stop herself from taking in his lean form. Did he always eat like this? If so, where did he store it all?

"You like what you see, *mi ánde*?" Brann's eyes twinkled with mirth at catching her checking him out.

"Yes and why wouldn't I? You're a good looking man." Hy almost missed the flinch at the end of her statement. "What's wrong Brann? Why did you flinch?"

He shook his head, but when he looked at her again, Hy made sure to focus all of her energy on getting him to explain what had caused that flinch.

Brann leaned back in his chair, his legs stretched forward and crossed at the ankle and his arms crossed on his chest.

"Do you know what your asking, *mi ánde*? I don't think you do, but yet I want to tell you. I have this ever increasing need to tell you everything."

Hyacinth evaluated the man in front of her — she seemed to do that a lot — and searched for an answer to his question. No, she didn't think she had a clue about what she was asking. Hell, she wouldn't be asking if she did, right? She felt a need to delve into his secrets and to prod at his emotions. She wanted to know him, all of him, and she was surprised to find an awareness inside of herself that he hid so much of himself from her... from the world. Hy struggled with the concept of what she felt. It was a sort of knowing. And, part of that knowing, was the knowledge that this man would never hurt her. She could trust him. After Tom, she hadn't thought she would ever feel ready to make the jump into romance again, but with Brann, it felt right.

"Then, tell me," she leaned in and whispered.

Brann leaned forward over the table and overwhelmed Hy's senses. Time stood still and she couldn't have said how long they sat there and soaked in each other.

"I think I will. This is not the time I would have chose, but I'm tired of the distance between us." Brann stood and moved his chair directly beside her own.

Once he was seated, he leaned into her and took her hands in his own. He seemed to really like holding her hands, it made Hy giggle to think about it. Holding hands seemed like something only small children did. But, the feelings that the contact sent through her body, were no where near innocent. The connection between them crackled with electricity. It sent fire through her stomach and shivers down her spine. Need. Lust. Love. Passion. All of those words could only describe a fraction of the intense bond she felt building between her and Brann.

"*Mi lys*, do you believe in the paranormal?"

"What, like tarot readings and seances and the like?"

Brann shrugged. "That is a part. But, I was talking about creatures that defy what you've been taught? Creatures like…" Brann gripped her hands tighter. "…like dragons."

A bark of laughter escaped before Hy could suck it down. Pulling her hand from Brann's she clapped it over her mouth.

"I'm sorry, so sorry, Brann. You're being serious, aren't you?"

He nodded in agreement.

"I read a lot, Brann. We've talked about a lot of sci-fi and fantasy, so you know I enjoy it. Maybe even a bit more than the average person. But, to believe in such things? That's a bit too large of a leap for me I think." Hy slid her chair away from Brann and put some distance between them.

Every inch that separated them felt like an ocean, but she had a feeling that she would need the distance for clarity.

Brann looked around the restaurant and leaped to his feet. Throwing some cash on the table, he gripped her hand and pulled Hyacinth with him. She barely had time to grab her clutch and wrap, before he was pulling her through the restaurants door.

"I'm sorry about dinner, *mi kjerlighet*, but we're going to need some privacy and some space."

Chapter 6

*L*ove conquers all.

Hy's head swam as Brann drove them across town and out onto the country roads. Within fifteen minutes he was turning down a bumpy dirt road. Another fifteen minutes found them turning onto a rural drive that meandered through a densely forested area. She had no idea where they were and prayed that there was cell service in case... well, in case of anything.

The silence was deafening as Brann concentrated on steering the truck and keeping them on the uneven road. Hyacinth absently twined the chain of her clutch over the fingers of one hand while her other absently traced the rearing dragon design of her pendant.

Dragons? Did she believe in such things? It wasn't inconceivable for creatures such as those in myth to be real and what she had always read stated that all myths were seated firmly in reality. So, what reality could influence the belief in dragons? at some point had there been throwbacks to the dinosaurs? Or, did it have some basis on elephants and rhinos or even large lizards?

Of, course if Brann was speaking of the paranormal from a broad understanding, there were more than the fire breathing, gold hoarding lizards that she always loved reading about to consider. The truth was Hy was a dragon junkie, Sam knew this and that was why she bought her the necklace she now wore. So, was the necklace the reason Brann had asked her about dragons? Was it something totally unrelated to large lizards that he needed to tell her?

The more important question might be, why wasn't she freaking the hell out? She and Sam had spoken often about the desensitization of their culture and how it was taking more and more to cause a reaction in the patrons of the arts. Was she desensitized? Was that the reason behind the fact that she willingly let Brann put her in his truck and drive away or was there something much deeper leading her actions when it came to the man sitting beside her?

Her mind swirled around the known facts and always came back more confused than before. Thoughts of her cell resurfaced. The small electronic device had always been a safety net, but with Brann, she didn't feel as if she needed it. She may not know much about the man, the odd direction the evening had taken was proof of it, but her gut told her she was safe.

Anticipation raced through her as they rounded a curve into an open area. A cabin settled on the bank of a pond or lake — it was difficult to say in the dark. The whole scene was bathed in moonlight and the lake appeared to be on fire as the moonlight reflected off the mirrored surface of the still water.

Hy knew that something momentous was about to happen. She could feel it in every cell and her nerves sparked to life as Brann drove around to the back of the cabin. He parked and sat for long moments staring out over the water.

"Brann? I'm not sure how much more my nerves can take."

He sighed with a weariness that spoke of a great weight resting on the man's shoulders.

"I'm sorry, *mi kjerlighet*, I know this must seem strange. I'm sorry to scare you."

"Oh, I'm not scared. Nervous, yes. Curious, definitely."

"All right. I've been thinking on the drive here about how to tell you. I think it's best to do it quick and to do that it's best to show just you."

Brann turned in his seat and leaned over the console that separated them. He stopped inches from touching his lips to hers.

"*Mi lys*, I tried to postpone this, to give us time… to give me time to find the others, but Marc was right, Fate decides when the time is right."

His lips covered hers in a slow exploration. Hy felt as if she was drowning in sensation, but as Brann kissed her a connection was forming and her mind was opening to the larger universe. Something inside of Hyacinth was changing. She could pinpoint the exact moment the changes inside of her had begun; it was that moment she had looked into the deep blue eyes that had obsessed her dreams and her waking moments too. Meeting Brann had begun a chain reaction inside of her and now, she needed to understand why.

Brann reluctantly pulled away. Shifting back he looked into her eyes. They were both breathing heavily and neither seemed to want to make the first move to the next part of their relationship. Brann seemed almost fearful and it made Hy want to tell him to forget about the whole thing. She hated seeing the uncertainty in his eyes. Reaching up, she stroked her fingers along his jaw until they reached his hair. The silky strands twined around her fingers as she moved them behind his ear.

"I can wait, Brann."

His large hand covered hers where it tangled into his hair. He held it there and closed his eyes for a few moments.

"No. It is time." He finally pulled away and opened the truck door.

Brann raced around the truck and had her door open before she could even blink.

"Come, *mi kjerlighet*." He offered her his hand and helped her jump from the large truck. "Just remember, I will never hurt you. Please do not be afraid of anything that I show you tonight. I won't let anything happen to you… ever."

Placing a last quick kiss on her lips, he led her towards the shoreline. As Hy's eyes adjusted she could see that the body of water stretched out farther than she could see. There were no other houses that she could see. No docks, other than the one for this cabin, anywhere along the shoreline. Between her clearing vision and the moonlight, she was able to make out much of her surroundings and that helped a lot.

The man she had come to love stopped about ten feet from the water. "Stay here," he whispered before darting off into some shadows.

Several minutes passed in silence. Not total exactly, as Hy could here the water lapping against the dock and the banks. A breeze blew through the nearby trees causing the dry leaves to rustle as they danced across the ground. Creatures scurried in those trees and fish splashed in the water. The sounds of nature surrounded her, grounded her, and gave Hy a sense of homecoming. She was home here in this wildness.

A flickering light danced across her eyelids, causing her to realize that she had closed them. She opened them to find Brann approaching from a small shed that was further down the water's edge past the dock. A torch now lit up the night from where it was grasped in his large hand and she adjusted to her expanded ability to see. Cataloging the new images that assaulted her mind. A shirtless Brann stopped a few feet away from her and placed the torch in a stand that had been set into the ground to hold similar torches in the past.

Brann stepped into the circle of light created by the torch. He braced his feet shoulder width apart and let his arms fall to his sides. Hy watched as he tipped his head back and stared into the night sky. After about a minute of watching him, Hyacinth's gaze began tracing a path down his body. She absorbed every inch of skin that was exposed without his shirt. It was shocking that she couldn't detect goosebumps on the exposed flesh. It was February for God sakes and the air had a briskness to it. Granted it was milder than normal, but not enough to go without a shirt and jacket. But, Brann stood as if he had no cares about the cold.

"Hyacinth, remember, I won't hurt you. My goal is to protect you from anyone or anything that would hurt you. No, watch me."

His head tipped forward and he focused on Hy. "Fra leirre till brann."

His last words boomed across the clearing and echoed off of the cabin. The breeze picked up and waves began to beat against the shoreline with increasing force. As the air picked up, Hy could feel bits of dirt and droplets of the water hitting her face. A second passed as she took it all in. The air surrounding them seemed to warm and solidify. That was when Brann began to shimmer... he went in and out of focus and with each view of clarity his skin appeared to be covered with more and more blue scales that reflected both moonlight and firelight. When the blue covered all of him that she could see, the shimmer flashed bright and raced from his head to his feet. Brann stretched his arms wide and as the shimmer slid over his arms, a leathery blue material draped down from them. A flare blinded her and when she could once again see, Brann... she knew it was him, but he looked so different... stood in front of her his arms outstretched to show her large leathery wings supported by cartilage and bone. His face had changed, too. It was now covered by blue scales. His eyes had become larger and his nose had sunken into a mere bump with large nostrils. His mouth seemed normal enough, although she was thinking it had become wider. He looked like some of the cosplayers that came around Sam's shop — like a six and a half foot tall lizard man with a wing span twice as wide.

Hy knew her mouth had dropped open at some point,

but no matter how hard she tried it wouldn't close and allow her to speak. Although, she wondered if it might be better to scream. Logically, she had a brief notion that she should scream and run. The huge ocean blue eyes that glowed with silver flecks and a ring of silver that outlined the now slitted pupil were unnatural... but familiar. Her inner-self told her to run to him, to hug him, and tell him all was well. Those alien eyes held the same fears and concern that Brann had worn before he stood in front of her.

One wobbling step at a time she advanced. The wings folded into the body, but the scale covered man remained. He reached out one arm, his fingers were covered by scales like the rest of him and his nails had lengthened into claws only a fraction longer than some of the long nails Hy had seen women wear. He turned his hand over and pressed a single claw — sharp side down — under her chin until her mouth finally closed.

Hyacinth swallowed. "Brann?" She was finally able to force through her dry lips.

"Yes, *mi sjelevenn*. I am a Drahgue, a lizard shifter that became the basis for the human dragon myths."

"May I touch..." Hy felt the blush rush her cheeks and her eyes dropped to the ground in between them.

Brann's response was to carefully grasp her hand in his own and to lay her hand flat over his heart. "You are my sjelvenn, Hyacinth. My light and breath. You never have to ask."

Her fingertips traced the individual scales. Each was

distinct but tightly woven to create a protective barrier.

"What do you think, *mi kjerlighet*?"

"I don't know. My brain is still processing."

"Are you afraid?"

"No, never."

"Then what is going on in that beautiful mind of yours?"

"Everything… and nothing." Hyacinth laughed and stepped back. She had never been good at thinking clearly around this man — this Drahgue.

"Can you change at will?"

"Of course. I used a spell of sorts, the words I said at the beginning; they slowed the process and allowed you to see the change. Normally, it's faster than the eye can even register."

"It didn't appear to hurt." Brann shook his head no in confirmation. "The wings… can you fly? Where did they go?"

Hy reached out for his hand and Brann anticipated her desire and lifted his arm. She walked slowly around him and he turned as well which allowed her to see all of him clearly in the light of the flame. She hadn't noticed before, but he had also removed his shoes, which was a good thing since he now had large claws extended from his toes. The scale-covered foot, still remained much like his human foot should look like. His dress pants didn't look the worse for wear and although his legs seemed to have filled out the material a bit more than before, they appeared to be human in structure. He no longer had a belly button — the thought brought a laugh from her lips and Brann smiled in return — he also no longer had nipples. Instead, his pectorals were covered with large plates. Where the rest of his body seemed to be covered with a woven network of scales, his pecs had one single large scale on each one. As she stepped around to his back she could see large muscled ridges that arced out and down his arms. She could envision these ridges interconnected and locking together to create the structure for his wings. But, Hy couldn't see his wings anywhere.

"Where are your wings?"

"They disappear when they are not needed. It would be difficult to fight with them spread at all times. The wings are terrific in the air, but on the ground they become cumbersome. Here…" Brann reached around and pulled her to his front. He settled her into the crook of his left arm and held his right aloft. "… it takes a bit of practice, but I can bring them out separate or together."

Hy watched in awe as the leathery material that she'd noticed earlier began to appear and drape down to the ground from his arm. Brann stretched out his wing as it materialized until it was held at its full wingspan.

"It's amazing." Hy gushed as she turned her head up to look into Brann's face. "Your face is different too."

Hyacinth shivered as a cool night breeze blew in off the water behind them.

Brann pulled his arm in towards them, but instead of the wing disappearing, he arched it into a curve that surrounded them completely.

"They are flexible and make good wind blocks too." Brann chuckled at her mesmerized expression. "As for my face, it adjusts to allow for me to breathe fire."

"What?" Hyacinth jerked in his arms. For the first time, she felt a tingle of fear and she wanted to run away from the flames that she saw arise in her inner eye.

Brann held her in place, "*Mi lys*, I won't hurt you. It only comes when I call it. See?"

He turned his face up and away from her. She could still clearly see all of his features, but as smoke began to curl from his nostrils, it was carried away in the wind. Hy was overwhelmed by everything, but she couldn't stop watching as the man she knew she cared for puckered up his now thinned out lips and blew a small stream of fire into the night sky.

Hyacinth asked many more questions and Brann provided answers, then at some point near dawn, Brann changed back to the man she had worked with for months and they went inside to sit in front of a roaring fire.

Brann had just left her to fetch some drinks and Hy was taking the time to really absorb the large open floor plan of the cabin. It was strange, but it seemed larger on the inside than the outside. She knew it couldn't be true and pushed the through off to the side. Instead, she inventoried every corner that her eyes could reach and she found it perfect. The colors were a mix of greens and blues that reminded Hy of the ocean.

She had always wanted to take a trip to the coast, but life had never worked out for it to happen. Brann's home embodied everything she had always dreamed of when thinking of the ocean.

"Here you are." He handed her a glass of juice and settled on the sofa to drink his own.

"Brann, I'm sorry about the lost data. Now that I know why you're looking for those people you've had us searching for, it makes my heart hurt at the thought of the wasted time."

She turned to him. They both faced each other on sofa cushions and Brann's arms were stretched out across the back of the head rest. Without a second thought, she weaved her fingers in his own.

"You could not have known. I was afraid of your reaction to the truth. It's been centuries since the old ones scattered our race to the four winds. I've been searching since the death of my own parents fifty years ago. If it's one thing us Drahgue understand, it's patience. When you live as long as we do, you learn the value of waiting for the perfect moment."

"Um, Brann?"

"Yes, *mi lys*."

"How old are you?"

Brann laughed and with a tug he had her pulled into his arms and sitting on his lap.

"Drahgue are immortal, *mi kjerlighet*. We can live as

long as we desire. We can be killed, but it is not easy. Generally, if we lose our *sjelevenn*, we chose to die."

"One, that is not an answer. Two, what are all of these phrases you keep using. I didn't know a lot about you, so never really stopped to worry about them. I just assumed it was some other language and I guess it is, just not any of them that I was thinking."

Brann chuckled. "Most are just pet names. You know how important you are to me, yes?"

Hy nodded and focused on his lips as he spoke.

"Well, *sjelevenn* means soul mate. I knew from the moment that I met you that you were mine. *Jeg gir mitt hjerte og ild min drage, á beskytte deg, det er min pilkt á beskytte det som er funnet.*"

Hyacinth sucked air in quickly and made shocked sounds as she fought to stop the tilting of her world as Brann's words entwined her in an invisible vise.

"Breathe, *mi ánde*. I am here and you are safe." Brann rubbed her back soothingly and snuggled her head onto his chest. "I don't expect you to feel the same, Hyacinth. I hope you do, but it is a decision that you have to make."

While stroking his fingers through her hair, Brann continued in a quiet voice.

"To answer your question, I'm two hundred and seventy-three years old. I was born just after my parents moved with their families to the United States. I told you a bit about the fighting and the unexplained deaths that led to fear and dissension between the *Familliens*. We lived with our families, but we learned and worked within our *Famillien*. You noticed my blue scales that mark me as part of the Bláa Famillien. There are three other recognized *Familliens* — *Guul, Gronn*, and *Rodd*. But, at the time of the upheaval, a fifth *Famillien* was born. A single female child was born with iridescent scales. Much of the knowledge about this child has been lost, but my grandparents who had been alive at the time of her birth said that many were fearful of her powers. Between the loss of so many Drahgue to an unknown foe and the birth of this child, my grandparents said that many families chose to leave our homeland and hide."

Brann's deep voice soothed Hy and she felt her breathing relax into easy breaths. At the words he had spoken in his language, something had shattered around her. It felt as if a hard shell that she had worn her entire life had finally shattered and she was able to shed the weight of it. Learning to breathe again without that weight had taken her a bit to achieve. Hy wasn't afraid. She knew her heart. But, now she also knew something else as well...

"Brann, I'm Drahgue. My parents left me when I was three years old to save me."

His head snapped down as he pulled her back. For a moment, he seemed to be the fish out of water for a change.

"What do you mean, Hyacinth?"

"You are my *sjelevenn*. You were the only one who could break the spell that they had placed over me. The spell forced my Drahgue characteristics down so that I could hide as a human."

"But, why would they be fearful?"

Hyacinth lifted silver and gold glowing eyes up to Brann. Tears had begun to fall as the memories surfaced. In human appearance, she had been three years old, but in reality she had already lived 12 years when the spell had taken away all of her power and magic that made her Drahgue. It hadn't been truly gone. Just barricaded behind a protective wall.

"Why, Hyacinth? It will not change how I feel, tell me."

"I am *Skkimrennde*. I was born with iridescent scales." Hy picked up on Brann's shock, but he didn't interrupt her. "When I was born, my parents knew that the others would be afraid of me and want me dead. Much of their history had been lost. Everyone that they lived with were all from their own generation, I didn't remember why, but my parents and the others were all less than a hundred years old. So, they didn't know what my being *Skkimrennde* meant, but they loved me unconditionally and knew they had to protect me. They were on the run for twelve years. They had been right and the others were fearful and did want me dead, unfortunately, that meant that they didn't let my parents go easily. When I was twelve they made the decision and approached a warlock to cast a spell that would make me human. It was cast so that if I ever found my soul mate and he spoke the beginning of the *Knytte*, the spell would be broken and my memories would return. All my parents wanted was for me to have a chance at a happy life."

Brann continued to stare into her glowing eyes for several minutes. He finally moved to grasp her face between the palms of his large hands. His thumbs stroked along her temples and Hy closed her eyes in contentment. She was sure that eventually everything would hit her and she would have her freak out, but for now she felt as if she finally completely knew herself. That she was home. She prayed the Brann wouldn't push her away. She had a feeling that it would be more than a simple broken heart if he did. This man was her soul mate and for the Drahgue that was something extremely special. They had a quality to them, a naiveté that only a child could hold true. She knew there was more that she didn't know – information that she hadn't understood or that her parents had deemed her too young to know at the time. So, for now, all that mattered was whether Brann could accept her as she was, as *Skkimrennde* – an iridescent Drahgue female.

"Oh, Hyacinth." Brann laid a row of light kisses across her forehead before he began speaking again. "*Det er min pikt á beskytte.* It is my duty to protect you. *Du er ná pusten som fans flammene og lys som styrer min vei.* You are now the breath that fans the flames and the light that guides my way. I have loved you from the moment I pushed your mouth closed for the first time and I will love you until the day we are no more."

"Oh, Brann, I love you too. My god with the blue eyes." Hyacinth laughed. "No, my dragon with the blue eyes."

Brann pulled her into his embrace and proceeded to kiss her until she was dizzy and breathless.

"Say you'll be mine, *mi lys og ánde*. There is so much that we both need to learn, but it won't change my feelings for you and I want you to be officially mine. I want everyone, especially that *faenen drittsikk* ex of yours, to know that you are not available."

Words surfaced from the deepest depths of her past, words that she knew because they were a part of her heart and soul.

"*Á allddri vaerre atskkiltt igjenn.* Always, Brann."

They sealed the pledge with a passionate kiss.

Hy wasn't sure where her plan had derailed, the night had changed so quickly, but she wouldn't change anything. She had the man of her dreams and was ready to make a life with him.

"*Mi kjerlighet.*" Brann whispered against her lips.

"*Mi sjelevenn.*" Hy whispered in return.

Chapter 7

Wedding Bells.

In the days since that night, Brann had made her dreams come true… each and every one of them. They had spent the last year searching for others like themselves, other Drahgue. There had been few successes, but they weren't giving up. Brann had taken a few trips to search for answers in regards to her being *Skkimrennde*. She had remained behind at Brann's insistence. He was afraid that others would react the same as her parents people had and she had respected his thoughts on the matter. They had found very little.

Brann had worked with her to try and determine what her powers would be. Brann's own was working with the power of water. He could control it and morph it to his needs. Other than having more and more deja vu moments and sensing things before they happened, Hy hadn't been able to work with any of the four elements that Brann knew about. Even Mr. Trollmann, who she had learned was actually a warlock, could sense anything about her. He said that to him, she still appeared completely human.

"Damn it all to hell, Hy!" Sam yelled from the doorway of the dressing room. You are not going down that fucking aisle without some make up on and your bling."

Hy chuckled at her friend. It was a year to the day since she had learned what Brann and herself were. The man had insisted that she be given time to adjust to everything before he would agree to perform the *Knytte*. Now, she had finally worn him down. Sam had helped Hyacinth re-plan Operation Cupid's Arrow and she had seduced that man to an inch of his life. Bringing them both to the edge and then pulling back. It hadn't been easy for her, so she knew that Brann had to be frustrated beyond endurance, but he had agreed to her insistence that they not have sex until they were bound together.

It had taken her longer than she thought, but he had finally agreed to a Valentine's Day wedding.

"Sam, you know Brann likes me natural."

Hy turned to find her friend standing in the doorway, arms crossed and toes tapping.

"Come on." She pleaded. "Just some eye make-up to enhance those gorgeous eyes of yours. You only get this day once and it should be perfect. That photographer has been paid a lot of money to make you look beautiful, but you should still give him some help, Hy."

"Fine, you twisted my arm, but eye makeup only." Hy turned to look into the mirror and watched Sam approach slowly.

Her friend lifted her arms over her head and laid something cold against the skin of her neck. Hy looked down to find the dragon pendant that she had worn a year ago. However, this time, it had a second dragon twined around the first. The second was made of opal stones and the two together appeared to be embracing in mid-flight. It was strange how the original dragon on its own had appeared to be rearing in protection, but together the whole feeling of the pendant changed.

"Oh, Sam, you shouldn't have."

"Don't worry I didn't. That addition would be from the groom."

She stroked the two dragons and thought of her soon to be husband. They would be bound by both Drahgue law and human law. Hy couldn't wait. She jumped to her feet and turned to hug her best friend tight. Sam still didn't know the truth of what she and Brann were, but someday Hy knew she would tell her. Until then, she would watch out for her friend and maybe see if she could aim one of Cupid's Arrows her way. Hy wanted Sam to be as happy as she was.

"Enough of that. You don't want your eyes to be puffy." Sam pushed Hy back into the seat and proceeded to do her eye makeup and force her to put on some lipstick as well.

"Your mission if you choose to accept it is to not have a speck of this remaining by the end of the evening." Both women laughed.

"I love you, Sam. You are the sister of my heart and I'm glad we found each other."

"Right back at you, lady. Now let's go get ya hitched."

*

The wedding had gone beautifully. Just a few of Brann's family and friends, Mr. Trollmann, and Sam were in attendance. But, after the vows had been exchanged, the small assembly had returned to the cabin for a blowout of a reception. She would remember the day for all time and was glad that Sam had talked her out of a quickie wedding at the justice of the peace.

Now she waited on her and Brann's bed deep inside of a cavern where he joked his horde was stashed. He had carried her over the threshold and ushered her into the large adjacent bathroom to this bedroom where he left her to get ready for bed. Brann had waggled his eyebrows as he backed from the room, claiming that he needed to get a few things sorted.

Hy leaned against a pile of pillows as she waited for the man to return. The exhaustion began to settle over her as the events leading up to this day finally caught up to her. She hovered on the edge of sleep when a clanging racket woke her from her light doze.

"Faen mi. I am one lucky dragon." Brann said as he stepped over a metal tray that now lay at his feet with delicious looking fruits, crackers, and cheeses surrounding it.

"Who needs food, when I have you to gobble up, *mi ánde.*" Brann's knees hit the bed and he inched forward to lay a kiss on her mouth.

Hy pushed at his chest. "Not until the *Knytte* has been

performed, Brann."

"Then you shouldn't have worn that nightgown, *mi lys*."

"So, you like? Sam thought it was too prudish."

"Sam's an idiot. It's perfect." Hy laughed as his eyes roamed her body. "Up on your knees, *mi kjerlighet*." His eyes once again punctuated his words with additional meaning.

Hy struggled to a sitting position and slapped his arm. "Behave you."

"Around you? Never." Brann said as he knelt across from her on the bed.

He laid a silken red cord beside his leg and a small dagger beside the cord. Hy shivered. She wasn't sure if it was fear of the knife and what she had to do, or in anticipation of what she knew would come after the *Knytte*. Heat rose on her cheeks and Brann once again had to press her mouth closed.

"You ready, *mi sjelevenn*? Ready to be bound to me for eternity?"

"Eternity won't be long enough to spend with you, Brann." Hy laid her hands on her knees and Brann copied the stance.

They took each other for a few seconds before Brann picked up the dagger and cut a small slice into his left hand. He offered the knife to Hy and she mimicked the slice on her own palm. Brann grasped her left hand in his own, pressing the two bleeding wounds together, he wrapped the cord several times in an infinity type of formation across the backs of their hands. They both reached out in unison to place their right palm flat against the others chest over their hearts.

Hy felt the power rise and begin to entwine their destinies as they began reciting the *Knytte* one line at a time.

Jeg gir mitt hjerte og ild min drage,

I give my heart and the fire of my dragon,

á beskytte deg,

for your protection,

det er min pilkt á beskytte det som er funnet.

for it is my duty to protect what has been found.

With each passing second her palm burned with more and more heat as they finished the first stanza. Brann brought their bound hands to his lips and blew his breath across them. The burning sensation became so intense that it took everything Hy had to bring their hands up to her own lips and blow. The fire flared and hey recited the remaining stanza.

Du er ná pusten som fans flammene og lys som styrer min vei.

You are now the breath that fans the flames and the light that guides my way.

Brannen melds det som en ang ble delt.

The fire melds what was once split.

Á aldri vaerre atskilt igjen.

To never be separate again.

The last line reverberated through the cavern and Hy felt a bridge between her and Brann lock into place. She knew his feelings at that moment and knew that he loved her as much as she loved him. There had been moments leading up to the wedding when she had worried about Brann being faithful. Her old insecurities reared their ugly heads and she had bashed them back with everything she had. She loved Brann and knew he would always keep her heart safe. Now, she could read his heart and know that for the truth it had always been. Brann was not Tom. It killed her to even think of him while in her marriage bed, but Hy didn't want any remaining doubts. From this moment on, it was her and Brann against all that would try to tear them apart and she needed to have unwavering trust in that fact. She had a feeling that their trust and love would be tested in the future and it needed to be rock solid. To be melded together so that nothing could split them apart again. She had found the other half of her soul.

"I love you, *mi sjelevenn*."

"It is official, Operation Cupid's Arrow is a success."

"Yes, *mi kjerlighet*, even a dragon's hide can be pierced by Cupid's arrow."

About the Author

Josette Reuel spent many years in the corporate world writing stuffy computer software manuals, until one day a shape-shifting dragon kidnapped her and dragged her off to be his destined mate... as the words flowed onto the page, she realized that it was time to fulfill her lifelong dream of becoming a published author.

An avid reader from her earliest memories, Josette enjoys many genres; however, her current passion is anything Romance. Her love of Fantasy and the Paranormal tends to come out in all of her writing with strong alpha heroes, each with a little something extra.

Josette writes paranormal romance of varying degrees of heat. She believes in LOVE in all of its forms and doesn't discriminate or sensor her muse. If you enjoy reading a love story, if you enjoy paranormal creatures, alpha males, and the heroes/heroines that change their lives, then how about giving her books a try?

Connect With Me Online

Twitter: https://twitter.com/JosetteReuel, @JosetteReuel

Facebook:
https://www.facebook.com/josette.reuel
https://www.facebook.com/JosetteReuelAuthor
https://www.facebook.com/JReuelNewRelease
https://www.facebook.com/groups/dasreachwarriors

Google+: https://plus.google.com/+JosetteReuel

Pinterest: http://www.pinterest.com/josettereuel/

Instagram: https://www.instagram.com/josettereuel/

Goodreads: https://www.goodreads.com/evanlea

BookBub: https://www.bookbub.com/authors/josette-reuel

Web site: http://JosetteReuel.weebly.com

Books By Josette Reuel

Dásreach Council Novels

Book 1: Finding the Dragon

Book 2: Accepting the Bear

Book 3: Releasing the Panther

Book 3.5: A Second Life As A Bear

Draghue Dragon

1.0: Love Burns

Holiday Pack

1.1: Wolves for the Holiday

1.2: Wolves for the Holiday

Gwar'Arth of Karhu Ridge

1.0: Subtle Magic

Spencer's Helpline

1.0: Shift or Treat

Also watch for Josette's stories featured in multi-author anthologies.

Did You Enjoy This Book?

If you enjoyed reading this book, I appreciate your help in letting other readers enjoy it, too.

Recommend it. Help others find this book by recommending it to friends, readers groups, and discussion boards.

Review it. Tell others about why you liked this book by reviewing it at your retailer, Goodreads, and/or your blog. Reader reviews help authors continue to be valued by retailers and help new readers make decisions when choosing books. I appreciate all feedback and look forward to seeing your review.

Love Burns

Made in the USA
Middletown, DE
29 March 2024